Gopher the Chauffeur

Lesley Sims

Illustrated by David Semple

Gopher drives a golden car.

She's chauffeur to the Queen.

I have to take tea with the Mayor. I'm really not that keen.

They see a sign.

"I love the sea!" the Queen agrees.
"Quick, turn around the car."

They drive along a country lane.

Gopher picks up pace.

A gust of wind blows washing free.
It flies in Gopher's face!

Now Gopher can't see where to go.
She drives across a farm.

They swerve around
a big, brown cow...

...and end up
in a barn.

"I'm sorry, Ma'am," poor Gopher cries.

A hen flies off her leg.

"Don't worry so," the Queen replies.
"Look! I've just caught an egg!"

They leave the farm and drive along.

Soon, they can see the sea.

Three seagulls hover overhead.
KER-SPLAT!
Oh dearie me!
QUE EN1

Again they can't see where to go.

They bounce across the sand...

...and splash through waves as
Gopher steers the car back onto land.

An octopus has hitched a ride
on top of Gopher's head.

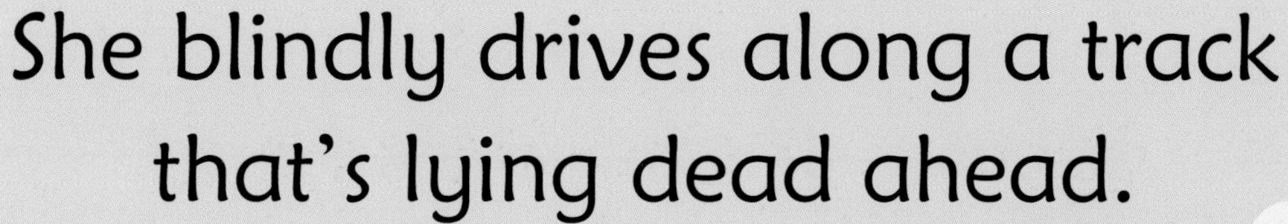

She blindly drives along a track
that's lying dead ahead.

They whirl around, then up and down.
They sway from side to side.

“Yippee!” the Queen shouts out in glee.
“It’s one fantastic ride.”

They get to town,
both safe and sound.
Poor Gopher looks quite green.

"I'm ready!" smiles the Queen.

Starting to read

Even before children start to recognize words, they can learn about the pleasures of reading. Encouraging a love of stories and a joy in language is the best place to start.

About phonics

When children learn to read in school, they are often taught to recognize words through phonics. This teaches them to identify the sounds of letters that are then put together to make words. An important first step is for children to hear rhymes, which help them to listen out for the sounds in words.

You can find out more about phonics on the Usborne website at **usborne.com/Phonics**

Phonics Readers

These rhyming books provide the perfect combination of fun and phonics. They are lively and entertaining with great story lines and quirky illustrations. They have the added bonus of focusing on certain sounds so in this story your child will soon identify the long *o* sound, as in **gopher** and **blow.** Look out, too, for rhymes such as **leg** – **egg** and **green** – **Queen**.

Reading with your child

If your child is reading a story to you, don't rush to correct mistakes, but be ready to prompt or guide if needed. Above all, give plenty of praise and encouragement.

Edited by Jenny Tyler
Designed by Sam Whibley

Reading consultants: Alison Kelly and Anne Washtell

First published in 2022 by Usborne Publishing Ltd., 83-85 Saffron Hill, London EC1N 8RT, England. usborne.com